JAN 1967 NO. 2

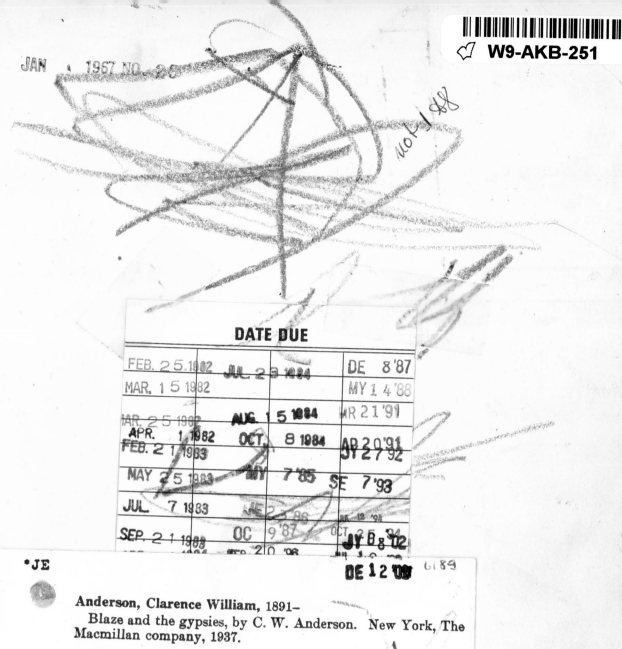

DATE DUE

FEB. 2 5 1982	JUL 2 3 1984	DE 8 '87
MAR. 1 5 1982		MY 1 4 '88
MAR. 2 5 1982	AUG. 1 5 1984	MR 21 '91
APR. 1 1982	OCT. 8 1984	AP 20 '91
FEB. 2 1 1983		JY 27 '92
MAY 2 5 1983	MY 7 '85	SE 7 '93
JUL 7 1983	JE 25 86	JUL 12 '94
SEP. 2 1 1983	OC 9 '87	OCT 25 94 JY 8 02

*JE   DE 12 00   6189

Anderson, Clarence William, 1891–
    Blaze and the gypsies, by C. W. Anderson. New York, The
Macmillan company, 1937.

    [56] p. illus. 25½ᶜᵐ.

    Illustrated t.-p.

1. Horses—Legends and stories.   ɪ. Title.   37—4883

Library of Congress   PZ7.A524Bl
————— Copy 2.
Copyright A 104612   [37d3]   RBP

BLAZE AND THE GYPSIES

By C. W. Anderson

Blaze
and the Gypsies

BY C. W. ANDERSON

THE MACMILLAN COMPANY • NEW YORK

MACMILLAN NEW YORK • LONDON

A Division of The Crowell-Collier Publishing Company

1962

Library of Congress
catalog card number: 62-14795

Printed in the United States of America
Sixteenth Printing, 1962

THE MACMILLAN COMPANY, NEW YORK
BRETT-MACMILLAN LTD., GALT, ONTARIO

Blaze
and
the Gypsies

Billy was a little boy who had a pony
named Blaze that he loved very much.
Billy and Blaze and his dog Rex
were always together. Every day the
three of them would go for long
rides through the woods.

One day they were going at a swift gallop along a road, pretending they were in a race. Rex could hardly keep up with them.

Suddenly around a turn in the road they met a covered wagon driven by gypsies.

The gypsies stopped and asked Billy many questions about his pony and his own name and where he lived.

When he got home from his ride his father told him the gypsies had been there. They wanted to buy Blaze. At first Billy was frightened. Then he knew that his father would not sell the pony he loved so much.

During the night Rex went to the window and growled. Billy thought he smelled some animal and told him to be quiet. He did not want him to wake his family.

In the morning when Billy went down to the stable to feed Blaze he was frightened to see the stable door open. And when he got there and found Blaze gone, he was heartbroken.

Blaze always came when Billy called.
Now Billy called and called, as loudly
as he could. There was no sign of Blaze
anywhere.

All day long he walked through the country looking for Blaze. He asked everyone he met about his pony. That night he and Rex came home very sad and discouraged.

Billy was too unhappy to play or to go anywhere. Rex knew something was wrong.

Many, many miles away Blaze was being
led behind the gypsy wagon farther
and farther from home. The gypsies
followed back roads where they would
not be seen.

When the gypsies camped for the night, they tied him to a tree and left him. Blaze was tired and hungry, and he longed to be back home.

One morning he saw the gypsy coming toward him with a large stick in his hand. He was frightened. When he reared up the rope broke. He was free at last. He started off at a gallop for home.

The gypsy jumped on one of his horses and chased after Blaze. A man coming along the road tried to stop him, but he turned off the road and jumped a high wall and raced across the fields.

When the gypsy tried to go over the wall too, his horse would not jump. He stopped so suddenly that the gypsy sailed over the horse's head, and landed on the ground.

Blaze was in strange country, but he knew where home was, for a horse does not often get lost. Over fences and through fields he ran. He was so happy to be free again.

It was dark in the woods, but he knew
his way and kept right on toward home.

He came to a large stream. There was no bridge, so Blaze jumped in and swam.

He was very tired when he reached the other side but he started off again.

Soon he came to a road he knew. Billy and Blaze and Rex had taken many rides on this road. He forgot about being tired and started off at a fast gallop.

All these days at home Billy was
thinking of Blaze and missing his pony.
They had had no news of him. Billy's
mother had made his favorite cake for
him, but Billy couldn't eat. He was too
unhappy.

Then one day while they were eating
lunch, suddenly there was a noise at the
window. Billy looked up and there was
Blaze looking in at him.

It was hard to say who was happier,
Billy or Blaze. Blaze was muddy and
dirty, but he looked beautiful to Billy.

Billy led him back to his stable. He fed him and petted him and cleaned him. How happy they were to be together again!

Billy's father promised to get a strong
lock for the stable door the next day so
that Blaze would be safe. Billy had
missed Blaze so much he could not bear
to leave him. He took a pillow and
blankets down to the stable that night
and slept there. He was so happy that
he dreamed all night of the many happy
rides he and his pony and Rex would
take together.